Princess Penelope's Parrot

HELEN LESTER

Illustrated by LYNN MUNSINGER

HOUGHTON MIFFLIN COMPANY BOSTON

For *Alison Abbott,* a great educator and friend —H. L.

For *Linda* —L. M.

Walter Lorraine (wл) Books

Text copyright © 1996 Helen Lester
Illustrations copyright © 1996 by Lynn Munsinger

Library of Congress Cataloging-in-Publication Data

Lester, Helen.
  Princess Penelope's parrot / Helen Lester ; illustrated by Lynn
Munsinger.
    p. cm.
  Summary: An arrogant and greedy princess's chances with a handsome
prince are ruined when her parrot repeats to him all the rude
comments the princess has made.
  CL ISBN 0-395-78320-8   PA ISBN 0-618-13845-5
  [1. Princesses—Fiction. 2. Parrots—Fiction. 3. Behavior—
Fiction.] I. Munsinger, Lynn, ill. II. Title
PZ7.L56285Pr 1996
[E]—dc20   95-53266
                                        CIP
                                        AC

Manufactured in China
SCP   10 9

Princess Penelope's birthday was always a big occasion,
and this year was no exception.

Princess Penelope's dress had ruffles on its ruffles
on its ruffles.

Her presents were fabulous.
Roller blades studded with jewels.

A bathing suit woven from
rare peacock feathers.

A sixteen-wheeler.

The cake was seven layers high and
made with genuine llama's butter.
The top of the cake was decorated with
a golden cage. Within that golden cage
was a beautiful parrot.
"GIMME," said Princess Penelope,
her mouth stuffed with cake.
"GIMME, GIMME, GIMME."

Quickly her servants stood one
on top of the other, plucked
the golden cage from the top
of the cake, and presented it.

"MINE," said the princess. "MINE, MINE, MINE."
Dribbling cake crumbs, she zoomed off to her chamber
with the cage.
Then she waited for the parrot to say something.
The parrot said nothing.

"TALK, BIG BEAK," demanded Princess Penelope.
The parrot said nothing.

"SPEAK, OR I'LL RATTLE YOUR CAGE."
The parrot said nothing, and Princess Penelope grew annoyed.
"ALL RIGHTY THEN, I'LL PUT YOU ON A BALL AND CHAIN."
The parrot looked miserable but said nothing.

Gritting her teeth, the princess hissed,
"LOOK, BIRDBRAIN, I'M ABOUT READY TO PLUCK YOUR
FEATHERS OUT ONE BY ONE."

Still the parrot said nothing.
Furious, Princess Penelope marched right up to the cage,
stared at the parrot nose to beak, and yelled,
"WHY DON'T YOU JUST GET LOST, KNOTHEAD?"

But the parrot did not get lost.
It stood in silence, nibbling forlornly
on the precious few birdseeds
the princess flicked its way.
Princess Penelope glared at the parrot,
snarling, "STUPID BUZZARD."

One day Princess Penelope received
a message that young Prince Percival
would be stopping by her palace on his
way to build sandcastles
at the beach.

Although they had never met before, Princess Penelope
had long ago decided that she would marry Prince Percival
when she grew up. He was the richest prince
in the land. Not just a little rich.
But Rich, RICH, **RICH.**
She could just picture herself as Mrs. Prince Percival.
She'd have diamonds sparkling from every toe and finger
and a crown so heavy it would fold her ears.

The most precious of silks would cloak her right up
to her royal nose.
Maybe her royal nose would have a golden nose ring.
She would make hundreds of lists for her servants.

Then she'd settle back on her velvet pillows to eat caviar
cones and watch a twenty-foot TV all day long.

But enough dreaming.
Now she must get ready
to make a fine impression on the prince.
She chose her poofiest dress,
arranged a new hairstyle,
and struggled into her
highest heels.

As she clippy-clopped about, tidying her room (leaving out
only her most expensive toys), she came across the parrot.
Stupid buzzard, she thought.
Would the prince be impressed by this useless bird?
Absolutely not. Never.

So she hid the parrot behind the curtains.

There.

Now everything was perfect.

Princess Penelope put on her sweetest smile, sat upon her throne, and waited to dazzle the prince.

KaLUMP. KaLUMP. KaLUMP.

Princess Penelope put her hand to her ear.

This must be her prince!

KaLUMP. KaLUMP. KaLUMP.

She could just imagine him galloping up on his fine white horse.

KaLUMP. KaLUMP. KaLUMP.

Prince Percival galloped into Princess Penelope's chamber.

No horse.

But impressive feet.

And nice shoes.

Whoosh. Prince Percival bowed deeply and held out a huge bouquet of roses.

"GIMME," said the parrot from behind the curtain.
"GIMME, GIMME, GIMME."
Prince Percival gulped and handed over the roses.

"MINE," squawked the parrot.

"MINE, MINE, MINE."

Prince Percival's eyebrows twitched. How could someone with such a sweet smile say such rude things?

"TALK, BIG BEAK."

The prince scratched his nose and thought that just maybe he wanted to be somewhere else.

Then the parrot screamed,
"SPEAK OR I'LL RATTLE YOUR CAGE."
Cage? Cage? Prince Percival
felt trapped. As he moved toward
the door the parrot screeched on,
"ALL RIGHTY THEN, I'LL PUT YOU
ON A BALL AND CHAIN.
LOOK, BIRDBRAIN, I'M ABOUT
READY TO PLUCK YOUR
FEATHERS OUT ONE BY ONE."
That did it. Prince Percival bolted
out the door and galloped off.
KaLUMP. KaLUMP. KaLUMP.

Princess Penelope followed. Clippy-Cloppy.
Clippy-Cloppy. Clippy-Cloppy.
And the parrot flapped after them both, ball,
chain, and all. Up and down staircases, past
the birthday present room, and through the kitchen they
KaLUMPED and Clippy-Clopped and flapped.
As Prince Percival finally galloped out the
palace door into the safety of the green
fields the parrot called out,
"WHY DON'T YOU JUST GET LOST, KNOTHEAD?"
Prince Percival was delighted to do so and
didn't stop once until he'd made it all the
way to the beach.

In the palace doorway the parrot cocked its head at
Princess Penelope and cheerfully said, "STUPID BUZZARD."
Then it stepped out of the ball and chain and
flew away.
The prince and the parrot lived together happily
ever after.

Princess Penelope was horribly embarrassed.
But she got over it.
And in no time she went right to work in front of
her mirror, practicing her sweetest smile —
just in case the second richest prince in the land
should come her way one day.